ABUELO

by Arthur Dorros

Illustrated by Raúl Colón

HARPER

An Imprint of HarperCollinsPublishers

For Aldo and his *abuelo gaucho*, who inspired this story, and for the Redmond and Masuelli families, *para todos, con cariño*—A.D.

For Tito and Mily (the Horn family)—R.C.

When I was little,
Abuelo and I would ride
with the wind, *"el viento,"*
washing our faces.
We could ride anywhere.

We would ride into the clouds,
with the sky, *"el cielo,"*
wrapped around us.

If it rained, Abuelo showed me
how to use my poncho
to make my own house.
"*Tu propia casa*," he would say.

At night, we could see forever.

"*Mira*," look, he would tell me,

reaching his hands to the stars.

Sometimes I'd get off the trail.

Abuelo laughed, but not at me.

"That happens to everyone," he told me.

"*Es bueno reírse*," it is good to laugh,

he said to me as we found the trail again.

As we rode,

he would say to his horse and me,

"*Hablamos*," we talk.

To guide a horse
he did not use spurs.
He could guide with a touch,
or with how he leaned, or with his voice.

When we met a mountain lion,
Abuelo showed me how to stand.
There are many ways to be
strong, "*fuerte*," he said.

We stood as strong
as any mountain trees.

But one day, my family told me
we were moving to the city.
"*No te preocupes*," don't worry,
Abuelo told me, we could visit.

On the way to the city,
our bus bounced from here to there.
I thought we might be lost, "*perdidos.*"

Then I remembered Abuelo's laugh,
and I laughed.
We were not lost.
We arrived at our new home.

At first I could not see
the stars, *las estrellas*.

Then I saw one, and another,
and lights that were city stars,
and I could almost see forever.

On my first day of school,
a bully jumped at me.

I stood strong, *fuerte*,
like a mountain tree.

Little by little, I began to know the city.
It was wide in different ways, like *La Pampa*.
I talked with Abuelo, and we visited.